Dedicated to
friendship

Edie
Be Brave
Karen and Shanée

In a green leafy forest, in a burrow dug deep,
a small armadillo was curled up asleep.

"Dillo, Dillo, listen to me," his Mama said,
"Today, I want you to find termites for tea."

ANXIOUS
ARMADILLO

Karen Lord and Shanée Buxton

Trembling with fear, his body shook.
He opened one eye and took a look.

Shivering anxiously, he twitched his nose,
flicked his tail and uncurled his toes.

"Find termites on my own?" he said,
"I'm too frightened to go out alone!"

Cautiously he waddled, looking all around...

...past the mossy logs, lying on the ground...

...HE STOPPED!

"What's that I can hear? Something's **buzzing** in my ear."

Humming near some butterfly lilies, hovered a bird of beautiful blue.

Dillo closed his eyes tight, he knew just what to do.

Dillo flipped his head over, tucked in his ears, pushed his legs under to hide all his fears.

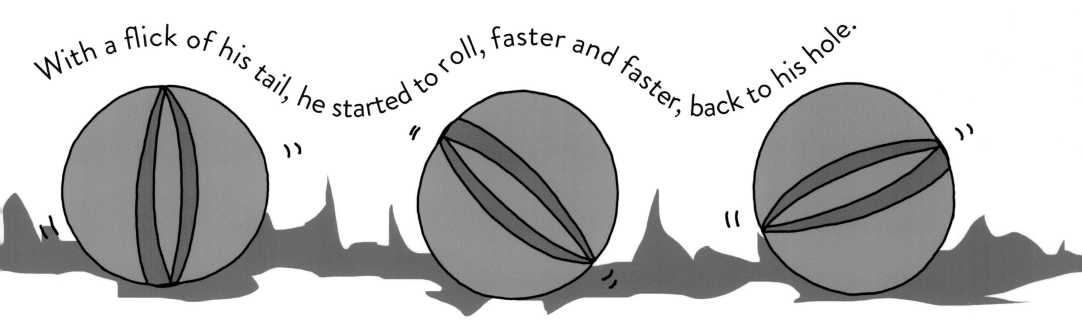

With a flick of his tail, he started to roll, faster and faster, back to his hole.

"It was just a humming bird, now come on be brave."

"But find termites on my own?" said Dillo, "I'm too afraid to go out alone!"

Cautiously he waddled, looking all around...

...past the mossy logs, lying on the ground...

...round the humming bird by the butterfly lily..

...HE STOPPED!

"What's that I can see... two **LARGE** scary eyes looking at me!"

Sitting on a gnarled tree trunk,
    was a frog with **BIG RED** eyes.

He croaked very loudly,
    giving Dillo a surprise.

"Dillo, Dillo," said Mama, "A tree frog won't hurt you!"

"But find termites on my own?" said Dillo, "I'm too worried to go out alone."

...under a low branch...

...HE STOPPED!

"What's that I can feel here? Something furry touching my ear."

Hanging from a twisted branch,
was a sloth upside down.

Dillo closed his eyes,
trying hard not to frown.

Dillo flipped his head over, tucked in his ears, pushed his legs under to hide all his fears

With a flick of his tail, he started to roll, faster and faster, back to his hole.

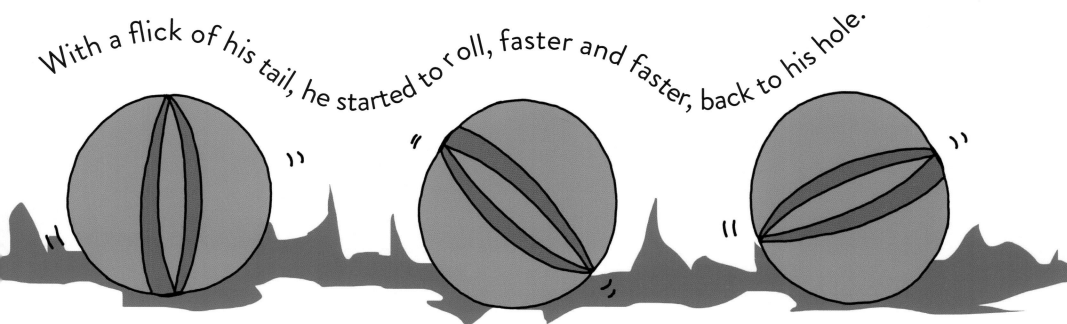

"Dillo, Dillo," said Mama,

"It's a sleepy sloth, be bold, you can do it!"

"But find termites on my own," said Dillo, "I'm too scared to go out alone!"

Cautiously he waddled, looking all around...

...past the mossy logs...

...round the humming bird...

...past the red eyed frog.....

...under the furry sloth on a low tree branch... by a muddy trail... **HE STOPPED!**

"What's that smell? It's very strong...

...**THERE'S DANGER,** something must be wrong!"

A smelly skunk was standing by a muddy trail.

Dillo closed his eyes...

...the skunk lifted his tail.

PHEW!

Dillo flipped his head over, tucked in his ears, pushed his legs under to hide all his fear.

With a flick of his tail, he started to roll, faster and faster, back to his hole.

"Dillo, Dillo," Mama said,

"It's a skunk, come on, you are doing so well!"

"But find termites on my own?" said Dillo, "I'm not sure, I can go out alone!"

Cautiously he waddled, looking all around...

...past the mossy logs...

...round the humming bird...

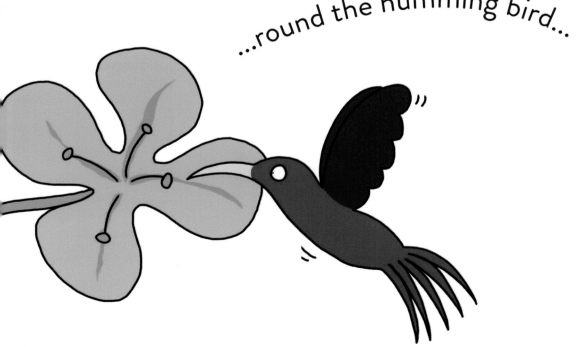

...past the red eyed frog...

...under the furry sloth on a low tree branch... near a smelly skunk by a muddy trail...

...to an opening lit by the sun.

With a flick of his tail, he started to roll and...............STOPPED!

Dillo opened his eyes, twitched his nose, flicked out his tail and uncurled his toes.

"Why am I anxious? What's wrong with me?" he said,

"It's my favourite...